THE
LION KING 1½

Bath New York Singapore Hong Kong Cologne Delhi Melbourne

Timon was not happy with his simple life in the meerkat village. Dig, dig, dig - that was all he ever did! And unfortunately, he wasn't very good at it. . . .

"TIMON!" Uncle Max yelled as Timon caused another tunnel to collapse.

"Not again . . . ," Timon's mum groaned.

To avoid more cave-ins, the meerkats decided to put Timon on sentry duty. His new job was to stand guard and watch out for hungry predators. But Timon began to daydream, and he didn't notice the approaching . . .

"Hyenas!" Uncle Max screamed as he and Timon ran for their lives.

After a narrow escape, Timon decided to leave the village. "I'm never gonna fit in here," he told his mum. "I gotta go." So Timon gave her a good-bye hug and set off to find his place in the world. But the little meerkat quickly realized he didn't know what he was looking for.

"Which way should I go?" Timon cried.

Just then, Rafiki the baboon appeared.

"You seek *hakuna matata*," Rafiki said with a chuckle. "Life without worry!" The mystical monkey pointed Timon toward a cliff called Pride Rock - then disappeared!

Timon began his journey to Pride Rock. As he walked in
the moonlight, he heard something moving in the tall grass.
Timon came face to face with - a warthog!
"Aaaaahhh!" he screamed.
"Aaaaahhh!" the warthog screamed back.

Once they were done screaming, Timon and the warthog introduced themselves. The warthog's name was Pumbaa, and he was looking for a home, too!

Realizing that they had a lot in common (they both ate bugs), the new friends set off together for Pride Rock. But Timon and Pumbaa quickly learned that finding the perfect place to live wasn't going to be easy.

"Oh, I give up," Timon groaned.

"But we still haven't found our dream home!" Pumbaa shouted.

And that was when they stumbled on the perfect spot - a beautiful oasis with plenty of yummy bugs to eat.

The two friends knew just what to name their new home. "Hakuna Matata!"

It wasn't long before Timon and Pumbaa had a new room-mate. A little lion cub named Simba had collapsed in the desert. They rescued Simba and invited him to live with them. The three friends played together every day and went to bed happy every night.

Many months passed. Then one day, everything changed. A lioness named Nala came to visit the oasis. And Timon and Pumbaa learned that Simba was really the Lion King! After Simba had left the Pride Lands, his evil uncle, Scar, had taken over as king - and all the animals were suffering.

Simba left the oasis to take his rightful place as king of the Pride Lands. "It's not *hakuna matata* without Simba!" Pumbaa sobbed. "We gotta go help our friend!"

But Timon didn't want to leave. "I've got everything I ever wanted right here," he said, crossing his arms.

So Pumbaa went off to follow Simba - alone.

It didn't take long for Timon to realize that he needed his friends to truly have *hakuna matata*. So he caught up with Pumbaa, and together they set off to help Simba. In the Pride Lands, they ran into . . .

"Ma! Uncle Max! What are you doing here?" Timon cried.

"Looking for you," his mum responded.

After a quick but tender reunion, Pumbaa pointed
to the top of Pride Rock. Simba was fighting with Scar -
and the wicked hyenas were about to ambush Simba!

"What do we do?" Pumbaa asked in a panic.

"I've got a plan," Timon said.

Just as the hyenas were closing in on Simba . . .

"Hey, what do you call a hyena with half a brain?"
Timon cried out. "GIFTED!"

The hyenas were so angry, they turned away from
Simba - and toward Timon and Pumbaa!

But it was a trap! Uncle Max had dug a hole - and
Timon and Pumbaa tricked the hyenas right into it. Timon's
plan worked!

"My son . . . the hero!" Timon's mum cried as the hyenas
tumbled down the hole.

After he had defeated Scar, Simba ran over to Timon and Pumbaa.

"I couldn't have done it without you guys," the Lion King said as he gave his friends a big hug.

Timon's mum was very proud!

"Let's go home, Ma," Timon said.

And that's just what they did! Timon led his mum, Uncle Max and all the other meerkats to their new home - the oasis.

"I gotta hand it to you," Timon's mum said. "This place has everything."

"Now that we're all here, it does!" Timon replied.

Hakuna matata!

Mufasa arrives just in time to save Simba. But when he asks Scar to help him get out of the valley, Scar throws Mufasa down the wall. The king is dead and Simba is very sad. Can you see the name Simba in this wordsearch? How many times can you see it?

SIMBA

A	Z	B	S	I	M	B	A
N	E	S	I	M	B	A	L
U	I	T	A	D	U	C	T
B	L	S	I	M	B	A	S
O	S	U	G	R	L	X	H
S	I	M	B	A	D	Z	W

Your answer is:

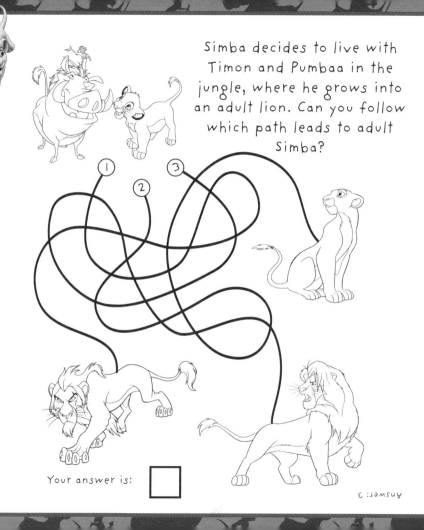

Simba decides to live with Timon and Pumbaa in the jungle, where he grows into an adult lion. Can you follow which path leads to adult Simba?

Your answer is: ☐

Answer: 3

The three friends live a "hakuna matata" life, which means "no worries". Can you colour the letters that spell hakuna in green and the letters that spell matata in red?

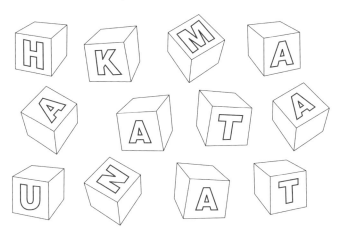

The lioness is actually Nala, and she's trying to find food for the animals of the Pride Lands. Can you join the dots to finish this picture of her? Then you can colour her in.

Nala tries to convince Simba to go back to Pride Rock with her and be king, but Simba wants to stay with his friends Timon and Pumbaa, and eat grubs and have fun. Can you count how many bugs there are?

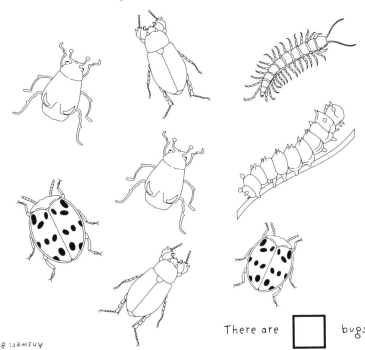

There are ☐ bugs.

Simba, Timon and Pumbaa all go back to Pride Rock to save the lions from Scar's evil rule. Can you help them find their way?

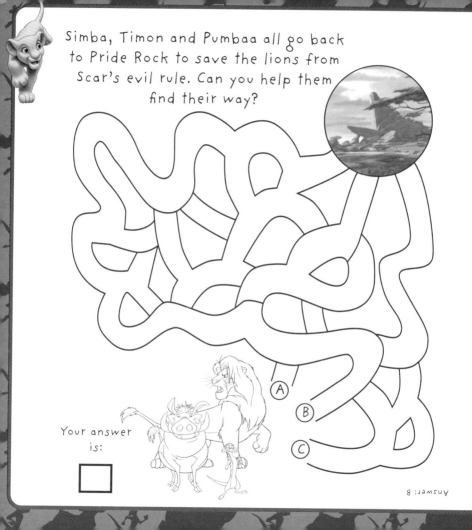

A

B

C

Your answer is:

When they arrive at Pride Rock, Timon and Pumbaa dress up to distract the evil hyenas, who are helping Scar. Can you colour them in?

Nala and Simba go for a walk to the waterfall.
Simba says he can never go back to Pride Rock
because of what happened to his father. Can
you colour this picture of them in using the
number code below?

1 = yellow   2 = brown   3 = orange   4 = red